CHARLES DICKENS

9 8 7 6 5 4 3 2 1
Digit on the right indicates the number of this printing

Library of Congress Control Number: 2011938031

ISBN 978-0-7624-4571-4

Running Press Book Publishers
A Member of the Perseus Books Group
2300 Chestnut Street
Philadelphia, PA 19103-4371

Visit us on the web!
www.runningpress.com

CHARLES DICKENS

THE COMPLETE NOVELS IN ONE SITTING

By Joelle Herr

RUNNING PRESS

PHILADELPHIA · LONDON

CONTENTS

Introduction

Even if you've never actually read a book by Charles Dickens, you're probably familiar with some of the characters he created: Ebenezer Scrooge, Oliver Twist, David Copperfield —over the past 150 years, these literary figures have become indelible pop culture icons.

Though it's true that his books have never gone out of print since their original publication, to say that the novels of Charles Dickens are "timeless" doesn't feel quite right given the fact that the time period in which they take place is practically a character in itself. Who doesn't automatically associate Dickens with the dank, rough-and-tumble streets of London during the gritty days of the

Industrial Revolution? The foundation of Dickens's works, however, rests firmly in the human experience, which transcends both time and place in the form of characters who are still relatable today, more than a century after they were written.

Let's face it, not many of us have the time—no matter how intrigued we are—to read all of Dickens's novels. Several of them clock in at around a thousand pages! That's where this book comes in handy—whether you want to get to know his collection of classics in a hurry or you're in search of a refresher course. Don't let its diminutive size deceive you. In this compact tome, you'll find summaries of all twenty of Charles Dickens's novels, along with some contemporary character descriptions, illustrations, and opening lines—efficiently organized for either digesting small chunks of information at a time or devouring the entirety in a single sitting.

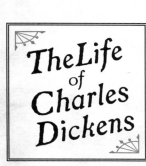

The Life
of
Charles
Dickens

Before we dive in, let's take a look (also somewhat condensed) at the life of Charles Dickens. As with many writers, his experiences greatly influenced the plots, themes, and characters of his works.

Charles Dickens was born in Portsmouth, England, on February 7, 1812, the second oldest child of John and Elizabeth Dickens. The family moved to London when

Charles was nine years old. His father was not very good with the family finances and was sent to debtor's prison when Charles was only twelve. While the rest of his family joined his father in prison, Charles spent three months working in a boot-blacking factory pasting labels on jars. It was a miserable time in the young boy's life.

After receiving an inheritance, Charles's father was

released from prison, and Charles was enrolled in a private school for three years. At the age of fifteen, he began working as a clerk in a law office, later deciding to become a freelance journalist reporting on various court proceedings. Near-farcical courtroom scenes detailing the absurdity and bureaucracy of the London judicial processes pop up in many of Dickens's works.

Dickens's first story was published in 1833, and his first novel, *The Pickwick Papers*, was serialized in 1836. That same year he married Catherine Hogarth, with whom he had ten children. Over the course of the next thirty years, he became one of the most prolific and best-selling writers of the Victorian Era.

In his later years, he embarked on several reading tours, including two in the United States. In 1857, he met and fell in love with Ellen Ternan, an actress, eventually separating from his wife the following year.

After a series of strokes, Dickens passed away on June 9, 1870, at the age of fifty-eight. An epitaph written at his death sums it up perfectly: "He was a sympathiser with the poor, the suffering, and the oppressed; and by his death, one of England's greatest writers is lost to the world."

The Pickwick Papers

(Serialized 1836–37)

"The first ray of light which illumines the gloom, and converts into a dazzling brilliancy that obscurity in which the earlier history of the public career of the immortal Pickwick would appear to be involved, is derived from the perusal of the following entry in the Transactions of the Pickwick Club. . . ."

The *Pickwick Papers* was Dickens's first novel, published when he was in his mid-twenties. The story follows the four members of the Pickwick Club on their adventures as they travel the English countryside. Naturally, they encounter a colorful cast of characters along the way, resulting in misunderstandings, lawsuits, imprisonment, and other hilarities, all of which they document in the "papers" of the title.

MAJOR CHARACTERS

Samuel Pickwick: The kind, elderly, and portly protagonist, founder of the Pickwick Club.

Nathaniel Winkle: A member of the club who fancies himself a good sportsman but is actually just the opposite.

Augustus Snodgrass: A member of the club who fancies himself a fine poet.

Tracy Tupman: An elderly, overweight, and generally unappealing member of the club who fancies himself a ladies' man.

EXCERPT FROM CHAPTER 28:

From the centre of the ceiling of this kitchen, old Wardle had just suspended, with his own hands, a huge branch of mistletoe, and this same branch of mistletoe instantaneously gave rise to a scene of general and most delightful struggling and confusion; in the midst of which, Mr. Pickwick, with a gallantry that would have done honour to

a descendant of Lady Tollim-
glower herself, took the old lady
by the hand, led her beneath the
mystic branch, and saluted her in
all courtesy and decorum. The
old lady submitted to this piece
of practical politeness with all
the dignity which befitted so
important and serious a solem-
nity, but the younger ladies, not
being so thoroughly imbued with
a superstitious veneration for the
custom, or imagining that the

value of a salute is very much
enhanced if it cost a little trouble
to obtain it, screamed and strug-
gled, and ran into corners, and
threatened and remonstrated,
and did everything but leave the
room, until some of the less
adventurous gentlemen were on
the point of desisting, when they
all at once found it useless to
resist any longer, and submitted
to be kissed with a good grace. . . .
As to the poor relations, they

kissed everybody, not even excepting the plainer portions of the young lady visitors, who, in their excessive confusion, ran right under the mistletoe, as soon as it was hung up, without knowing it! . . .

It was a pleasant thing to see Mr. Pickwick in the centre of the group, now pulled this way, and then that, and first kissed on the chin, and then on the nose, and then on the spectacles, and to hear the peals of laughter which were raised on every side; but it was a still more pleasant thing to see Mr. Pickwick, blinded shortly afterwards with a silk handkerchief, falling up against the wall, and scrambling into corners, and going through all the mysteries of blind-man's buff, with the utmost relish for the game, until at last he caught one of the poor relations, and then had to evade the blind-man himself, which he did with a nimbleness and agility that elicited the admiration and applause of all beholders. . . . When they all tired of blindman's buff, there was a great game at snap-dragon, and when fingers enough were burned with that, and all the raisins were gone, they sat down by the huge fire of blazing logs to a substantial supper, and a mighty bowl of wassail, something smaller than an ordinary wash-house copper, in which the hot apples were hissing and bubbling with a rich look, and a jolly sound, that were perfectly irresistible.

"This," said Mr. Pickwick, looking round him, "this is, indeed, comfort."

The Adventures of Oliver Twist

(Serialized 1837–39)

"Among other public buildings in a certain town, which for many reasons it will be prudent to refrain from mentioning, and to which I will assign no fictitious name, there is one anciently common to most towns, great or small: to wit, a workhouse. . . ."

MAJOR CHARACTERS

Oliver Twist: Orphaned at birth, the poor kid can't catch much of a break.

Fagin: Ringleader of a group of children he's trained as professional pickpockets.

Mr. Brownlow: Pickpocket victim who ends up taking Oliver under his wing.

Bill Sikes: Vicious thief who uses Oliver in one of his robberies.

Nancy: Girlfriend of Sikes who becomes sympathetic to Oliver— but at a dear price.

Rose: Instrumental in helping discover Oliver's past, she also uncovers the truth about her own.

Monks: For his own reasons,

works with Fagin in plotting against Oliver.

THE STORY

A woman in labor is found on the streets and brought into a workhouse, where she gives birth and then dies. Thus begins the life of Oliver Twist. After spending his first nine years in an orphanage, Oliver is sent to a workhouse, where he is mis-

treated and practically starved.
After daring to ask for more to
eat one day, he is sent off to
become an apprentice to the
local undertaker, Mr. Sowerberry.
One day, a fellow apprentice,
Noah Claypole, makes disparag-
ing remarks about Oliver's
mother, so Oliver beats him up.
Soon after, Oliver runs away and
finds himself heading toward
London.

Just before reaching London,

Oliver meets a boy his age, Jack Dawkins. Jack offers Oliver food and shelter in the home of his "benefactor," Fagin, who turns out to be a criminal, ringleader of a band of children thieves and pickpockets. Oliver doesn't find this out, however, until one day he is out with Jack and another kid and sees them pick the pocket of an elderly gentleman. Oliver tries to flee but is caught and nearly blamed for the crime—only getting off because an eyewitness says he's not the thief. Oliver is then taken in by the man whose pocket was picked, Mr. Brownlow, and leads a somewhat happy life for a while. Fagin is infuriated by Oliver's rescue, however, and sends two of his lackeys, Nancy and Bill Sikes, to kidnap Oliver and bring him back into the gang of outlaws. Oliver's disappearance leads Brownlow to believe that Oliver was in fact a thief all along.

Fagin sends Oliver along on a major robbery, where things go awry. Oliver is shot and left in a ditch. When he comes to, he goes to the nearest house, which happens to be where the bungled burglary took place. There, Mrs. Maylie and her niece, Rose, take Oliver in and offer him protection. Oliver spends a lovely summer with them in the countryside.

Enter the mysterious Monks. He is working with Fagin in a plot to destroy Oliver's chances of happiness and discovering his background. Nancy—now sympathetic to Oliver—arranges a meeting with Rose and Brownlow to inform them of the plot against Oliver. When word of this meeting gets back to Sikes, he is so infuriated that he murders Nancy.

Brownlow confronts Monks, who discloses the real reason behind his hatred for Oliver. He and Oliver are actually half brothers, and Monks wants to keep Oliver from claiming his share of the inheritance from their father, who died shortly before Oliver was born. Monks agrees to tell all he knows in exchange for immunity. Fagin is arrested and sentenced to death. Sikes accidentally hangs himself while trying to escape capture.

Another revelation occurs—
Rose is actually the younger
sister of Oliver's mother, making
her his aunt. She marries Mrs.
Maylie's son, Harry. Although
Oliver shares his inheritance
with his half-brother, Monks
still ends up dying destitute in a
prison. A happy ending is
achieved when Oliver is adopted
by Mr. Brownlow.

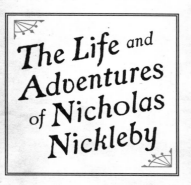

The Life and Adventures of Nicholas Nickleby

(Serialized 1838–39)

"*There once lived, in a sequestered part of the county of Devonshire, one Mr. Godfrey Nickleby: a worthy gentleman, who, taking it into his head rather late in life that he must get married, and not being young enough or rich enough to aspire to the hand of a lady of fortune, had wedded an old flame out of mere attachment, who in her turn had taken him for the same reason. Thus two people who cannot afford to play cards for money, sometimes sit down to a quiet game for love."*

MAJOR CHARACTERS

Nicholas Nickleby: The protagonist of the story who is loyal and very concerned with right vs. wrong. He is not without flaws, though, including a quick temper.

Wackford Squeers: Cruel and

greedy headmaster of the school where Nicholas goes to work.

Smike: Often ill and developmentally impaired charge of Squeers whom Nicholas takes under his wing.

Ralph Nickleby: Nicholas's rich and ruthless uncle who will do just about anything to thwart his happiness and success.

THE STORY

The beginning of the novel introduces us to Nicholas Nickelby, a young man from Devonshire whose father has just passed away, forcing him, his mother, and sister, Kate, to move to London to solicit help from his wealthy but heartless uncle, Ralph Nickleby. Ralph manages to find Kate a job with a milliner and Nicholas a position as assis-

tant to Wackford Squeers, headmaster of a Yorkshire boarding
school. The school turns out to
be a horrible place, where the
students are grossly mistreated
while their tuition goes straight
into Squeers' pockets. Nicholas
befriends Smike, a sickly young
man under the care of Squeers,
and becomes enraged when he
one day comes upon Squeers
striking Smike. Nicholas ends up
beating up Squeers and leaving

the school with Smike in tow.

After a brief stay in London with his sister and mother, Nicholas sets off with Smike to Portsmouth with the intention of becoming sailors. Along the way, however, they encounter the manager of a theatrical troupe who convinces them to join. They make their debut in a performance of *Romeo and Juliet*, with Nicholas playing Romeo.

Nicholas eventually returns

to London to aid his sister, whose reputation is being threatened by a man whose advances she rejected. Fed up with his uncle's selfishness, Nicholas rejects further assistance and heads to the employment office in search of work. There, he encounters Charles Cheeryble, a wealthy merchant who offers him a job.

Another person that Nicholas meets at the employment office

is beautiful young Madeline Bray. It's love at first sight for Nicholas. Unfortunately, she is being pressured to marry an elderly acquaintance of Ralph under the condition that her father's debts will be paid afterward. On the day of the wedding, however, Mr. Bray's guilt weighs so heavily on him that he dies, which frees Madeline from her obligation to marry the old man.

Meanwhile, Squeers has come to London to help Ralph in his quest against Nicholas. They attempt to take Smike from Nicholas by first kidnapping him and then presenting forged documents pertaining to Smike's parentage. Poor Smike has fallen ill with tuberculosis and ends up passing away in Nicholas's arms.

Then comes the big reveal —Smike had actually been

Ralph's son from a secret marriage. Upon learning this, Ralph commits suicide. Squeers is arrested and sent to Australia. Nicholas marries his love, Madeline, becoming a partner in the Cheeryble business and moving back to Devonshire, where they live happily ever after.

The Old Curiosity Shop

(Serialized 1840–41)

"*Night is generally my time for walking. In the summer I often leave home early in the morning, and roam about fields and lanes all day, or even escape for days or weeks together; but, saving in the country, I seldom go out until after dark, though, Heaven be thanked, I love its light and feel the cheerfulness it sheds upon the earth, as much as any creature living.*"

MAJOR CHARACTERS

Nell Trent: The innocent orphan child who pays the ultimate price for the mistakes of the adults in her life.

Grandfather: Nell's grandfather, who is well-meaning but indulges in a secret addiction that leads to his—and ultimately Nell's—destruction.

Kit: Nell's only friend, a young boy who works in Grandfather's shop.

Daniel Quilp: Deformed and evil moneylender who relentlessly pursues Nell and Grandfather.

Dick Swiveller: Initially enlisted by Nell's brother to marry her in order to gain her supposed fortune, he ultimately chooses good over evil.

THE STORY

Nell Trent is an orphan who is being raised by her grandfather, proprietor of the Old Curiosity Shop. She leads a very lonely existence, her only friend being young Kit, who works in the shop. While Grandfather truly cares for her, he suffers from a secret gambling addiction, a habit for which he is continuously borrowing money from Daniel Quilp, a grotesque and villainous moneylender. When Quilp learns that all the money he has loaned has been lost in gambling, he seizes the shop and kicks Nell and her grandfather out on the streets. Grandfather suffers a breakdown, forcing Nell to become his caretaker as they wander the countryside.

Meanwhile, Nell's selfish and wayward brother, Frederick, is unaware of his grandfather's gambling addiction and convinced that there is money stashed away for Nell. He enlists the help of his friend Dick Swiveller to track down Nell and their grandfather so that Dick can marry Nell and therefore get to her supposed fortune. Even though he knows the truth of Grandfather's financial circumstances, Quilp delightfully aids Frederick and Dick in their hunt.

Dick undergoes a transfor-

mation of character while under
the employ of Quilp's lawyer,
however, going from mindless
follower to someone concerned
with right and wrong. He later
helps prove the innocence of Kit,
who had been framed for robbery, and eventually marries a
poor and mistreated maid also
working for Quilp's laywer.

On their journey, Nell and
Grandfather encounter a variety
of characters, including an

impoverished schoolmaster and members of a traveling puppet show troupe. When they finally reach the safety of a country village, Nell is so exhausted by the journey that she dies. This is one of the most controversial deaths in all of literature as it caused an outcry from readers who wanted Nell to have a happy ending.

Barnaby Rudge

(Serialized 1841)

"In the year 1775, there stood upon the borders of Epping Forest, at a distance of about twelve miles from London—measuring from the Standard in Cornhill, or rather from the spot on or near to which the Standard used to be in days of yore—a house of public entertainment called the Maypole; which fact was demonstrated to all such travellers as could neither read nor write (and at that time a vast *number both of travellers and stay-at-homes were in this condition) by the emblem reared on the roadside over against the house. . . ."*

Barnaby Rudge was Dickens's first attempt at writing historical fiction. It takes place in 1780 London during the Gordon Riots. Responding to the Papists Act of 1778, which eased many of the restrictions placed on Catholics in Britain,

Lord George Gordon rallied his fellow Protestants to pressure Parliament to repeal the act, lest the Catholics return Britain to an absolute monarchy. On June 2, 1780, tens of thousands of people marched on Parliament. A mob mentality took over and rioting broke out. The novel follows a widely diverse cast of characters through these events.

MAJOR CHARACTERS

The Rudges: Barnaby, Mary (his mother), the mysterious man who turns out to be Barnaby Rudge Sr., and Grip (Sr.'s pet raven).

The Vardens: Gabriel (a locksmith), his wife, Martha, and daughter, Dolly.

The Haredales: Geoffrey (younger brother of Reuben) and Reuben's daughter, Emma.

The Willets: John (proprietor of the Maypole Inn) and his son, Joe.

Lord George Gordon: based on the real historical figure who helped organize the movement for the repeal of the Papists Act of 1778, resulting in the Gordon Riots of 1780.

Excerpt from Chapter 49

The mob had been divided from its first assemblage into four divisions; the London, the Westminster, the Southwark, and the Scotch. Each of these divisions being subdivided into various bodies, and these bodies being drawn up in various forms and figures, the general arrangement was, except to the few chiefs and leaders, as unintelligible as the plan of a great battle to the meanest soldier in the field. It was not without its method, however; for, in a very short space of time after being put in motion, the crowd had resolved itself into three great parties, and were prepared, as had been arranged, to cross the river by different bridges, and make for the House of Commons in separate detachments.

At the head of that division

which had Westminster Bridge for its approach to the scene of action, Lord George Gordon took his post; with Gashford at his right hand, and sundry ruffians, of most unpromising appearance, forming a kind of staff about him. The conduct of a second party, whose route lay by Blackfriars, was entrusted to a committee of management, including perhaps a dozen men: while the third, which was to go by London Bridge, and through the main streets, in order that their numbers and their serious intentions might be the better known and appreciated by the citizens, were led by Simon Tappertit (assisted by a few subalterns, selected from the Brotherhood of United Bull-dogs), Dennis the hangman, Hugh, and some others.

The word of command being given, each of these great

bodies took the road assigned to it, and departed on its way, in perfect order and profound silence. That which went through the City greatly exceeded the others in number, and was of such prodigious extent that when the rear began to move, the front was nearly four miles in advance, notwithstanding that the men marched three abreast and followed very close upon each other.

At the head of this party, in the place where Hugh, in the madness of his humour, had stationed him, and walking between that dangerous companion and the hangman, went Barnaby; as many a man among the thousands who looked on that day afterwards remembered well. Forgetful of all other things in the ecstasy of the moment, his face flushed and his eyes sparkling with delight, heedless of the weight of the great banner he carried, and mindful only of its flashing in the sun and rustling in the summer breeze, on he went, proud, happy, elated past all telling:—the only light-hearted, undesigning creature, in the whole assembly.

The Life and Adventures of Martin Chuzzlewit

(Serialized 1843–44)

"As no lady or gentleman, with any claims to polite breeding, can possibly sympathise with the Chuzzlewit Family without being first assured of the extreme antiquity of the race, it is a great satisfaction to know that it undoubtedly descended in a direct line from Adam and Eve; and was, in the very earliest times, closely connected with the agricultural interest."

MAJOR CHARACTERS

Old Martin: Elderly widower with possible paranoid delusional disorder.

Young Martin: The grandson of Old Martin who matures through the course of the proceedings.

Mr. Pecksniff: Self-proclaimed architect who mistreats his pupils.

Tom Pinch: Arguably the "true" hero of the story whose only fault is that he has trouble seeing the bad in others.

Anthony and Jonas Chuzzlewit: Greedy father and son who are ruthless in their quest to get to Old Martin's fortune.

The Story

At the head of the Chuzzlewit family is Old Martin, a wealthy widower whose family members are all angling to get his fortune. Old Martin is cared for by Mary, a young orphan girl who will be turned out on the streets upon his death (thus giving her ample motivation to take good care of him). The only family member not caught up in a desire to get a chunk of the fortune is Old Martin's grandson, also named Martin. He is more concerned with his growing love for Mary.

Young Martin is a pupil of Mr. Pecksniff, an architect and distant Chuzzlewit relation. Pecksniff is a greedy charlatan who treats his students poorly and lives a lavish lifestyle off of their tuition. Working for Pecksniff is Tom Pinch, a good-hearted but mistreated assistant of sorts. Once Old Martin gets wind of the budding romance between his grandson and Mary, he disinherits the young man, which eventually leads to his dismissal from Pecksniff's "school."

Young Martin, accompanied by friend Mark Tapley, ventures to America to start a new life. After being scammed into purchasing swampland, Martin and Mark nearly die of malaria. After they recover, they decide to return to London—Martin desires to make peace with his grandfather.

Upon returning, Martin finds that his grandfather is under the influence of Pecksniff, who is involved in a pyramid-like scheme with two other greedy Chuzzlewit family members: Anthony and Jonas. However, it turns out that Old Martin is merely acting, that he's actually wise to Pecksniff's despicable intentions. Much action ensues, including the suicide of Jonas, Pecksniff's financial ruin, and the revelation that Old Martin had intended all along for Young Martin to marry Mary. In the end, the good are rewarded with wealth and happiness while the bad get what they deserve.

The Five
Christmas
Novellas

A Christmas Carol

(1843)

"Marley was dead: to begin with. There is no doubt whatever about that. The register of his burial was signed by the clergyman, the clerk, the undertaker, and the chief mourner. Scrooge signed it."

MAJOR CHARACTERS

Ebenezer Scrooge: Miserly businessman whose catchphrase is "Bah, humbug!"

Bob Cratchit: Scrooge's underpaid and underappreciated clerk who nonetheless has a warm household and happy family life.

The Ghosts: Christmas Past, Christmas Present, and Christmas Yet to Come all have a few things they would like to show Mr. Scrooge.

Fred: Scrooge's nephew, who is treated horribly by his uncle but still has compassion for the cranky old man.

THE STORY

Welcome to the office of Mr. Ebenezer Scrooge. It is Christmas Eve, and he sits at his desk counting money while his employee, Bob Cratchit, dutifully works in the other room, freezing without a fire and wondering when he can go home to his family. Scrooge's nephew, Fred, stops by to invite his uncle to Christmas dinner the next day.

And two men ask Scrooge to donate to their charitable cause. All are met with scorn and a "bah, humbug" or two.

Alone in his room that night, Scrooge is visited by the ghost of his former business partner, Jacob Marley. Marley's ghost wears heavy chains and padlocks and tells Scrooge of the misery of his afterlife—punishment for his miserly and misanthropic ways. He hopes to spare Scrooge the same fate and lets him know that he will be visited that night by three more ghosts before the night is through.

First up is the Ghost of Christmas Past, who takes Scrooge back to his school. There, Scrooge sees himself as a child full of imagination and possibility. From there, they travel to his early adulthood, when Scrooge was a young apprentice to Fezziwig, a kind and generous man. Last stop with the Ghost of Christmas Past is a ball, where Scrooge sees his former fiancée, Belle, chastising him for being more concerned with money than love. The ghost then returns Scrooge, deeply moved by what he has seen, to bed.

The next visitor is the Ghost of Christmas Present, who shows Scrooge several different scenes that vary wildly in their sense of happiness and hope. Scrooge visits the Cratchit family as they prepare their meager holiday dinner. Scrooge is especially moved by the optimism of Cratchit's son, Tiny Tim, who, despite being disabled, brings great cheer to the house. Scrooge then visits the Christmas gathering that he had been invited to by his nephew, Fred. Scrooge must be changing

already because the former mis-
anthrope finds the party so
enjoyable that he doesn't want to
leave.

But he has one more visi-
tor—the Ghost of Christmas Yet
to Come. This hooded specter
shows Scrooge several scenes of
people reacting to a recent death.
Scrooge asks the ghost to tell
him who the dead man is, so the
ghost takes Scrooge to an open
grave, with a grave marker dis-

playing Scrooge's own name. Scrooge begs the ghost to let him live, promising that he will be a better person.

With that, Scrooge wakes up in his own bed and it is Christmas morning. Scrooge is so thankful for his second chance that he joyfully rushes out to the streets. He sends a huge turkey to the Cratchit house (and lets Bob know he's getting a big raise), and attends Fred's party.

Truly a changed man, he treats
others with warmth and compassion for the rest of his days.

The Chimes

(1844)

"Here are not many people—
and as it is desirable that a
story-teller and a story-reader
should establish a mutual understanding as soon as possible, I beg it
to be noticed that I confine this
observation neither to young people
nor to little people, but extend it to
all conditions of people: little and

big, young and old: yet growing up,
or already growing down again—
there are not, I say, many people
who would care to sleep in a
church."

MAJOR CHARACTERS

Toby (Trotty) Veck: A messenger by trade, very pessimistic and self-loathing.

Margaret (Meg) Veck: Trotty's daughter, who is engaged to be married.

Alderman Cute: A city magistrate who completely ignores the plight of the poor.

Sir Joseph Bowley: A member of parliament who fancies himself an advocate of the poor with really no understanding of their situation.

THE STORY

It is New Year's Eve and we are introduced to Trotty Veck, an impoverished ticket-porter (messenger) who is wallowing in pessimism—about himself, the world, and the people around him. He has allowed himself to buy into the misconception that the poor can only blame themselves for their condition and do not, therefore, deserve any aid or concern.

Over the course of the day, Trotty encounters several people— an alderman, an economist, a man pining for a return to the feudal system, and even a member of parliament—who reinforce his lowly position. They make him feel so worthless that he cannot even feel happy for his daughter, Meg, who is set to marry her fiancé, Richard, the next day.

That night, Trotty finds himself drawn to the chiming

bells of the church and ventures up to the tower, where he encounters the spirits of the bells and goblins who tell Trotty that he fell climbing the tower and that he's actually dead. They chastise him for his outlook and for not believing in progress and improvement. They show him a series of scenes from the future, including one in which Richard becomes an alcoholic and dies. Trotty then sees a vision of a destitute Meg considering drowning herself. Trotty is so upset that he begs for her safety, promising the spirits and goblins that their point has been taken and that he will change his attitude.

Trotty awakens to bells ringing in the New Year and with a new outlook on life, including the happy event of Meg and Richard's marriage that day.

The Cricket on the Hearth

(1845)

"The kettle began it! Don't tell me what Mrs. Peerybingle said. I know better. Mrs. Peerybingle may leave it on record to the end of time that she couldn't say which of them began it; but, I say the kettle did. I ought to know, I hope! The kettle began it, full five minutes by the *little waxy-faced Dutch clock in the corner, before the Cricket uttered a chirp."*

MAJOR CHARACTERS

John Peerybingle: Delivery man whose wife is much younger than he.

Dot Perrybingle: Wife of John, called Dot because of her small, round shape.

Caleb Plummer: Poor toymaker whose deception of his daughter is the result of good intentions.

Bertha Plummer: Caleb's daughter, who is literally blind and also kept in the dark as to the true nature of her surroundings.

Tackleton: Miserly owner of the toy factory.

The Story

The main theme of this Christmas story is deceit— and its destructiveness. John Peerybingle is a "carrier" by trade, who lives with his much-younger wife, Dot, and their infant child. John suspects that Dot might be having an affair with the mysterious lodger staying with them. On their hearth lives a cricket whose chirping songs fill the house with joy and warmth.

Meanwhile, Caleb Plummer is a poor toy maker who leads his blind daughter, Bertha, to believe that their meager home is beautiful and that his boss (and their landlord), Tackleton, is handsome and kind, as opposed to the reality of his old, cranky, and miserly self. So effective is Caleb's deception regarding Tackleton that Bertha has fallen in love with him, causing her to be upset upon hearing that he is engaged to marry May Fielding, a close friend of Dot.

John Peerybingle sits by the fire one night, his emotions stirred by suspicions regarding his wife. He contemplates killing the houseguest. The supernatural element of the story is the cricket, who speaks to John and convinces him of his wife's fidelity.

It is soon revealed that the lodger has been wearing a disguise and is, in fact, Edmond Plummer, Caleb's son, who had been May's lover years ago, before going off to sea. Dot had merely been facilitating meetings between the two. Edmond and May marry just hours before she was to marry Tackleton. John and Dot's marriage is as strong as ever. Bertha forgives her father for his deceit, realizing it was merely a sign of his love. And even the miserly Tackleton is transformed by the Christmas spirit into a joyous lover of life.

The Battle of Life

(1846)

"Once upon a time, it matters little when, and in stalwart England, it matters little where, a fierce battle was fought. It was fought upon a long summer day when the waving grass was green."

MAJOR CHARACTERS

Grace Jeddler: The elder Jeddler sister who has spent her life making sacrifices for her younger sister.

Marion Jeddler: Grace's younger sister who makes sacrifices of her own so that her sister may be with the man she loves.

Alfred Heathfield: Ward of Dr.

Jeddler who becomes a doctor to the poor.

Michael Warden: Spendthrift horse lover who undergoes a major change.

THE STORY

This "pretty story"—as Dickens himself described it—takes place in a tiny English village located on an ancient battle site. But the battles pertaining to this story take place within the characters themselves. At the heart are two sisters, Grace and Marion, who live with their father, Dr. Jeddler, and his ward, Alfred. Grace is the older sister who has basically been a mother to Marion. The story begins with a celebratory breakfast for Alfred's coming-of-age and Marion's birthday. After the party, Alfred leaves to figure out what he wants to do, but only after promising to return in six months to marry Marion.

Enter irresponsible degenerate Michael Warden, who claims to be secretly engaged to Marion after having spent time at the Jeddler household recovering from an accident. On the very day that Alfred returns to the village, a letter from Marion is discovered, detailing how she has eloped with Michael and left the country with him. (He had been advised to go abroad for at least six years after having wasted his family fortune on horses.)

Six years pass. Alfred marries Grace and they have a daughter named Marion. Michael returns to the village in order to sell his estate. It turns out that Marion had not eloped with him, after all. Marion had gone to live with a distant aunt, aware of Grace's love for Alfred and knowing that her absence would allow them to be together. In the end, the family is all reunited, and Marion marries a reformed Michael, who spent his six years abroad bettering himself.

The Haunted Man and the Ghost's Bargain

(1848)

"Everybody said so."

MAJOR CHARACTERS

Redlaw: A morose university chemistry professor who is visited by a phantom offering him a gift.

Milly Swidger: Filled with only goodness and compassion.

Tetterby family: All are affected by Redlaw's curse, which leaves them numb but also irritable and angry.

THE STORY

Redlaw is a solitary chemist who is haunted by painful memories of his past. One night, he is visited by a phantom and offered the gift of "forgetfulness." After some contemplation, Redlaw decides to accept the offer and the phantom reveals that Redlaw will pass along his forgetfulness to everyone he encounters.

It turns out that without painful memories, there can be no joyful ones, either. Redlaw becomes emotionless, a big nothingness that eventually turns into an inexplicable anger and irritability. Meanwhile, he passes his condition on to those around him—William Swidger, caretaker of the university where Redlaw teaches; and the Tetterbys, a neighboring family who rents a room to one of

Redlaw's students. The only person unaffected by Redlaw's curse is William's wife, Milly, whose painful memories of having lost a child have left her filled with warmth and compassion for others. It is through Milly that Redlaw finally finds redemption, realizing that without pain there can be no joy. Through her wisdom and guidance, everyone goes back to the way they were, except Redlaw, who has had a change of heart, finding compassion and love within himself.

Dombey and Son

(Serialized 1846–48)

"*Dombey sat in the corner of the darkened room in the great arm-chair by the bedside, and Son lay tucked up warm in a little basket bedstead, carefully disposed on a low settee immediately in front of the fire and close to it. . . . .*"

MAJOR CHARACTERS

Paul Dombey: Stern business-man, head of Dombey and Son, who wants nothing more than a son to continue his legacy.

Florence Dombey: Dombey's daughter, who, despite her efforts, is continuously rejected by her father.

Paul Dombey, Jr.: The golden

child and heir who is unfortunately very sickly.

Walter Gay: An employee at Dombey and Son who displeases his boss when he befriends Florence.

Edith Granger: Dombey's third wife, who is beautiful but haughty, and certainly does not marry Dombey for love.

James Carker: Conniving manager of Dombey and Son who proves to have no loyalty to his employer.

THE STORY

Dombey and Son begins with a childbirth scene. Paul Dombey's wife has just given birth to a son, Paul Jr. He already has a child, from his first marriage—a girl named Florence to whom he pays scarcely any attention. Dombey's life revolves around his business, which was started by his father and for which he must have a son for it to continue. Dombey employs a wet nurse, Mrs. Richards, to look after his son.

One day on an outing with Mrs. Richards, Florence is lost on the streets of London. After a brief kidnapping, Florence is found by Walter Gay, an employee at Dombey and Son, and returned to her home. A friendship blossoms between Florence and Walter.

Paul Jr. is a sickly child and dies when he is only six years old. At his death, Florence again tries to win her father's affection, only to be rejected. On top of that, her father sends Walter to work in Barbados, shortly after which news comes that the ship has been lost. Walter's uncle,

Solomon Gill, leaves his shop,
the Midshipman, in the care of a
friend, Captain Cuttle, to go in
search of Walter.

Dombey remarries a widow
named Edith, but she does not
love him and eventually runs off
to France with one of his
employees, James Carker. As
usual, Dombey takes his anger
out on Florence, who runs away
from home. She is taken in by
Captain Cuttle at the Midship-

man. Dombey sets out to look for Edith, who eventually leaves Carker, too.

Walter returns—he survived the ship's sinking, and he and Florence are married. Before heading off to sea for a year's voyage with his new bride, Walter writes a letter to Dombey, informing him of the marriage and asking that he consider reconciling with Florence.

Due to Carker's mishandling of the finances, Dombey and Son goes bankrupt. Dombey spends his days in solitude thinking of his lost daughter. After a year away, Florence returns with Walter and has a tearful reconciliation with her father, who lives with them and dotes on his grandchildren.

David Copperfield

(Serialized 1849–1850)

"Whether I shall turn out to be the hero of my own life, or whether that station will be held by anybody else, these pages must show."

MAJOR CHARACTERS

David Copperfield: Narrator of this story that is loosely based on Dickens's life.

The Peggotty family: The family of David's mother's servant, whom he looks upon as his own family.

The Micawber family: David boards with this kind but debt-riddled family while working in his stepfather's warehouse.

James Steerforth: David's fellow classmate at school in Canterbury.

Agnes Wickfield: Daughter of Mr. Wickfield, who provides David's lodgings while in school at Canterbury.

Uriah Heep: Untrustworthy and scheming employee of Mr. Wickfield.

Dora Spinlow: David's immature bride, whom he loves dearly, despite her ineptitudes.

THE STORY

David Copperfield's father dies before he is born, but his early years are spent in happiness with his mother and their servant, Peggotty. One day, Peggotty takes David to visit her family, and he meets her brother, Mr. Peggotty, and his two adopted children, Em'ly and Ham. Upon their return, David learns that his mother has married Mr. Murdstone, a severe man who beats poor David. David is eventually sent away to a horrible boarding school, where he befriends a boy named James Steerforth.

David's mother dies, upon which Murdstone sends David —still just a child—to work in one of his factories in London. While there, he boards with the Micawber family, who are friendly, though insolvent. Micawber is eventually taken away to debtor's prison. With no one to stay with, David runs away to Dover to find his aunt, Betsy Trotwood. She takes him in and treats him well, even sending him to a good school in Canterbury. While there, he lodges with Mr. Wickfield and his daughter, Agnes, who becomes David's friend. He also meets Uriah Heep, Wickfield's scheming and not very trustworthy clerk.

After finishing school, David decides to visit the Peggottys. He runs into Steerforth and invites him along. At the Peggottys, he learns that Ham and Em'ly are to be married. Back in London, David becomes an apprentice at a firm, Spenlow and Jorkins. David falls in love with Spenlow's daughter, Dora. Instead of marrying Ham, Em'ly elopes with Steerforth, prompting Mr. Peggotty to go looking for her.

David marries Dora, who turns out to be very inept at being a wife and running a household. David loves her anyway. Micawber proves central in exposing Uriah Heep's plot to ruin Mr. Wickham, and the Micawbers emmigrate to Australia. Em'ly is eventually found, and she and Mr. Peggotty also move to Australia to begin a new life. In a tragic twist of fate, Ham drowns trying to save a shipwrecked sailor off the coast of Yarmouth. The sailor, who also drowns, turns out to be Steerforth. Dora suffers a miscarriage and dies shortly thereafter, leaving David struck with grief. He travels abroad for three years, during which time he realizes his love for Agnes. They marry upon his return and have a wonderful and happy family.

Bleak House

(Serialized 1852–53)

"*London. Michaelmas Term lately over, and the Lord Chancellor sitting in Lincoln's Inn Hall. Implacable November weather. As much mud in the streets as if the waters had but newly retired from the face of the earth, and it would not be wonderful to meet a Megalosaurus, forty feet long or so, waddling like an elephantine lizard up Holborn Hill.*"

MAJOR CHARACTERS

Esther Summerson: A kind and loyal orphan of unknown parentage.

Lady Dedlock: Beautiful but bored wife harboring a secret from her husband.

John Jarndyce: Esther's guardian and proprietor of Bleak House, with an interest in the case

Jarndyce vs. Jarndyce.

Richard Clarton: Jarndyce's ward who becomes obsessed with the resolution of Jarndyce vs. Jarndyce.

Ada Clare: Jarndyce's beautiful ward, who captures the heart of Richard.

Mr. Tulkinghorn: Lady Dedlock's unscrupulous attorney.

THE STORY

There is a secret between Sir Leicester Dedlock and his wife, Lady Dedlock. Before they were married, she had a lover, Captain Hawdon, with whom she had a daughter. Lady Dedlock believes her daughter to have died, when, in fact, she was raised by her sister, Miss Barbary, as Esther Summerson.

After Miss Barbary's death,

Esther is sent to live with John Jarndyce at his estate, Bleak House, along with two other wards, Ada and Richard. John, Ada, and Richard are all involved in an obscure and complicated lawsuit called Jarndyce vs. Jarndyce, which has been knocking about the courts for many years. Once they settle into their new life at Bleak House, Esther begins to notice that Richard and Ada seem to be falling in love.

One afternoon, while meeting with her attorney, Mr. Tulkinghorn, Lady Dedlock recognizes some handwriting on a piece of paper as that of her former lover, Captain Hawdon. She investigates on her own and discovers that Hawdon (known as "Nemo") recently passed away, seemingly from an opium addiction—destitute and without friends. Tulkinghorn keeps a close eye on Lady Dedlock with the help of her discontented maid, Hortense. Lady Dedlock has a chance meeting with Esther at a church service. They determine the truth of their relation, though Lady Dedlock insists they must keep quiet.

Shortly after telling Lady Dedlock that he knows her secret, Tulkinghorn is shot. Detective Bucket comes in to investigate, and Lady Dedlock is a prime suspect. Her secret is revealed to her husband, who has a massive stroke yet is still able to communicate his forgiveness of his wife. Lady Dedlock flees, disguised in common clothes, and is later found dead at the cemetery gates where her former lover is buried. Meanwhile, Mr. Bucket deduces that Hortense is Tulkinghorn's murderer.

Back at Bleak House, Richard has become consumed by the lawsuit, determined to get a fortune from it, and secretly marries Ada. Esther contracts a serious disease (likely small pox) from which she recovers, but with a scarred face. She is engaged to her guardian, John Jarndyce, yet he releases her from her obligation upon realizing she is in love with a Dr. Allan Woodcourt. Still declaring her "prettier than ever," despite her scars, Woodcourt marries Esther.

Meanwhile, Jarndyce vs.

Jarndyce has come to an abrupt stop—the years of proceedings have consumed the money that was in dispute. At hearing the news, Richard collapses and dies shortly after of consumption. Ada gives birth to a boy months later, and both are taken in and cared for by Jarndyce.

(Serialized 1854)

"*Now, what I want is, Facts. Teach these boys and girls nothing but Facts. Facts alone are wanted in life. Plant nothing else, and root out everything else. You can only form the minds of reasoning animals upon Facts: nothing else will ever be of any service to them. This is the principle on which I bring up my own children, and this is the principle on which I bring up these children. Stick to Facts, sir!*"

MAJOR CHARACTERS

Thomas Gradgrind: Retired businessman and father devoted to fact and rational thought.

Tom Gradgrind: Gradgrind's son who becomes a selfish hedonist.

Louisa Gradgrind: Gradgrind's daughter who feels an emptiness in her life.

Sissy Jupe: Warm and happy daughter of a circus clown.

Josiah Bounderby: Dishonest mill owner and friend of Gradgrind.

Stephen Blackpool: Lowly mill worker struggling with his love for a fellow mill worker.

THE STORY

Thomas Gradgrind is a staunch believer in the power of fact and rationalism. He is a wealthy retired merchant in Coketown, England, who has founded a school based on his fact-based philosophy, where fancy, emotion, and imagination are frowned upon. His son and daughter, Tom and Louisa, attend the school, along with

Sissy Jupe, whose father is a clown with a traveling circus. Sissy is abandoned by her father and taken into the Gradgrind household for reformation (in Grandgrind's eye).

Gradgrind's friend, Josiah Bounderby, is a wealthy mill owner who declares himself to be an orphan and a self-made man. One day, one of his lowly workers, Stephen Blackpool, approaches Bounderby for advice. Stephen is in love with another mill worker, Rachael, but is not able to marry her because he already has a wife. Bounderby tells Stephen that he must remain in his marriage because he has no money, even though his Mrs. is a mean drunkard and known to disappear for weeks at a time.

After finishing school, Tom begins to work for Bounderby at his bank. Meanwhile Louisa agrees to marry Bounderby, though she feels no love for him. Sissy remains in the Gradgrind household to help with the younger children.

Time passes, and James Harthouse arrives in town to work under Gradgrind, who is by this time a member of parliament. Harthouse, an ambitious opportunist, takes a liking to Louisa and plans to seduce her.

Poor Stephen refuses to join

a union at the mill, so he is ostracized by his coworkers and then also by Bounderby when he refuses to act as his spy. Stephen plans to leave town, and Louisa gives him money to help him on his way. Tom assures Stephen that if he hangs around the bank the next couple of nights, he will also help him. Stephen hangs around the bank, but no one comes, so he leaves town. Soon after, the bank is robbed, and

Stephen is the main suspect.

After Harthouse proposes that they run away together, Louisa confesses her confusion to her father, collapsing in a state of exhaustion. Gradgrind realizes the mistakes made in raising his children—and that fact and rationalism are not always the best approach to life. Louisa never goes back to Bounderby.

On his way back to Coketown to declare his innocence, Stephen falls into an old mine shaft. He is pulled out but dies shortly after. At this time Louisa and Gradgrind realize that Tom was the one behind the bank robbery, and they help him escape the country with a traveling circus.

In the end, Bounderby is discovered to have abandoned his mother years ago—making him not only not an orphan but also a scoundrel. Sissy marries and has a big family of her own, which is joined by Louisa, who never married again. Tom dies abroad without contact with his family. And Gradgrind gives up his devotion to fact and rationalism, and redirects his political clout to aiding the poor.

Little Dorrit

(Serialized 1855–57)

"Thirty years ago, Marseilles lay burning in the sun, one day."

MAJOR CHARACTERS

William Dorrit: The "Father" of Marshelsea debtor's prison who is preoccupied with his gentility.

Amy Dorrit: "Little Dorrit," who was born in the prison and shows an intense loyalty to her father.

Mrs. Clennam: Invalid mother of Arthur who is keeping a very big secret.

Arthur Clennam: Returns to London after many years and finds himself intrigued by the mystery of a watch.

The Story

William Dorrit is a gentleman by birth but a poor businessman, resulting in his confinement to Marshelsea debtor's prison in London for many years. He lives there with his children, Fanny, Tip, and Amy, who was born in the prison. Amy is called Little Dorrit and is devoted to her father, earning money for the family by sewing. She eventually finds employment working in the household of the wealthy invalid Mrs. Clennam.

Mrs. Clennam has a son, Arthur, who has just returned from China, where he was living with his recently deceased father. On his deathbed, Mr. Clennam had given Arthur a watch and murmured "your mother," so naturally he assumes that his father meant for him to take the watch to her. But when he presents it she refuses to discuss its significance. Arthur is intrigued by his mother's kindness toward Amy and suspects she may have something to do with the mysterious watch. He investigates the Dorrit family and discovers that William Dorrit is actually heir to a great fortune, which enables him to leave prison.

Suddenly free and wealthy, William Dorrit takes his family

on an extended tour of Europe, where he and his children—with the exception of Amy—act with an air of entitlement and superiority. Mr. Dorrit dies in Rome, and Amy returns to London to live with her sister Fanny and her husband, Edmund Sparkler, who is a fool but wealthy. Edmund's stepfather turns out to have been involved in a fraudulent investment scheme, which leads to the Dorrits and Arthur Clennam losing their fortunes and being sent to Marshelsea prison.

Eventually, it is revealed to Amy that Arthur is not the son of Mrs. Clennam and that Amy (through her uncle, who was the friendly music teacher of Arthur's real mother) is actually the rightful heiress to the fortune. Amy chooses not to inform Arthur of this news because she is in love with him and wants the money to be his (by default). But wait, Arthur's business partner returns from abroad—their venture having been a success—resulting in a fortune for Arthur all his own.

Everyone is released from Marshelsea, and Amy and Arthur marry and go on to live a happy life.

A Tale of Two Cities

(Serialized 1859)

"It was the best of times, it was the worst of times, it was the age of wisdom, it was the age of foolishness, it was the epoch of belief, it was the epoch of incredulity, it was the season of Light, it was the season of Darkness, it was the spring of hope, it was the winter of despair. . . ."

MAJOR CHARACTERS

Dr. Alexander Manette: Once a highly respected doctor, he is wrongly imprisoned in the bastille for eighteen years.

Lucie Manette: Dr. Manette's daughter, who is very compassionate and devoted to her father.

Charles Darnay: A French aristocrat teaching French in London.

Sydney Carton: Bears a striking resemblance to Darnay, but is a bit of an apathetic drunk.

Marquis du Evrémonde: Darnay's uncle, who epitomizes the French aristocracy that the revolutionaries seek to abolish.

THE STORY

In 1757, Dr. Alexandre Manette attended to a dying girl who had been raped by the Marquis du Evrémonde, who had also murdered the girl's brother. Dr. Manette was afterward imprisoned in the bastille so that he would not tell anyone of Evrémonde's crimes.

Years pass, and it is 1775. Jarvis Lorry is accompanying

young Lucie Manette to Paris to be reunited with her father, whom she had thought was dead but who has just been released from prison. Delusional from his years in prison, Dr. Manette recognizes his wife in Lucie and begins to weep for all that has been lost.

Five years later, Lorry is summoned to testify in the trial of Charles Darnay, who is being tried for spying against England for France and the United States. Lucie and her father attend the proceedings. Darnay is acquitted only after one of his laywers, Sydney Carton, points out the resemblance between Darnay and himself—thus causing doubt related to the accuracy of eyewitness accounts.

Meanwhile, there is great social unrest stirring in France. The Marquis du Evrémonde runs down a peasant child in the streets of London and shows absolutely no remorse. His nephew, Darnay, arrives that evening and is so disgusted that he renounces his inheritance and says he plans to return to London for good. That night, the Marquis is murdered in his bed.

A year passes, and after spending quite a bit of time with the Manette family, Carton—in fact a bit of a degenerate drunkard—declares his love for Lucie but does not propose, knowing that she deserves better. He does promise her, however, that he will be there to help her in any situation. Darnay proposes to Lucie and they are joyfully married. He tells Lucie of his true identity as a French aristocrat the morning of their wedding.

The French Revolution breaks out in July 1789, and soon Darnay receives a letter from the former manager of his uncle's estate, who has been arrested and asks Darnay for help. Darnay travels to France but is quickly arrested. Lucie and her father travel to Paris. It turns out that because of his lengthy stay in the bastille, Dr. Manette is something of a hero to the revolutionaries, and he manages to get Darnay released. He is quickly arrested again, however, and at his second trial a letter written by Dr.

Manette while he was imprisoned is produced as evidence. The letter details the rape and murder that the Marquis du Evrémonde had committed years before. With this damning evidence, Darnay is found guilty for his uncle's crimes and sentenced to the guillotine.

Sydney Carton, ever in love with Lucie, gains access to Darnay in his prison cell, drugs and switches clothes with him, and assumes Darnay's identity—which he is easily able to do given the already-established physical similarities. Carton is executed in Darnay's place, while Darnay escapes back to England with his family.

Great Expectations

(Serialized 1860–61)

"*My father's family name being Pirrip, and my Christian name Philip, my infant tongue could make of both names nothing longer or more explicit than Pip. So I called myself Pip, and came to be called Pip.*"

MAJOR CHARACTERS

Pip: The orphaned narrator and protagonist who is terribly hard on himself and caught up in wanting to climb the social ladder.

Joe: Pip's uncle/father figure, the kindest character in the whole book.

Miss Havisham: The loony spinster mastermind.

Estella: The self-professed "heartless" beauty, the object of Pip's obsession.

Biddy: Intelligent and compassionate, but plain, which lands her in Pip's friends-only zone.

Orlick: The oafish and indisputable bad guy who attacks Pip's sister and later Pip himself.

Magwitch: The misunderstood

criminal with a heart of gold.

Compeyson: Former fiancé of Miss Havisham and partner-in-crime of Magwitch.

Herbert: Pip's BFF and eventual boss.

The Story

Philip Pirrip—"Pip"—is a young orphan who lives in the marshes of Kent in the care of his dictatorial sister and her husband, Joe, the village blacksmith. During the opening scene, Pip is visiting the gravesite of his parents when suddenly an escaped prisoner lunges at him, demanding food and a file to saw off the chain on his leg. Terrified,

Pip obeys and returns to the marsh with the items the following morning. Afterward, he feels immense guilt for having helped the escaped convict, who is eventually captured but says nothing to the police about Pip's aid.

One day a couple of years later, an arrangement is made for Pip to visit Miss Havisham, a wealthy, eccentric spinster who wears a tattered wedding dress and has all of her clocks stopped at twenty minutes to nine. Pip's aunt and uncle have high hopes that she intends to take him under her wing and help him become a "gentleman." On his first visit, Pip meets Estella, Miss Havisham's young ward, and is quite taken by her beauty, despite her condescending treatment of him. To Pip's great disappointment, Miss Havisham merely offers to aid in establishing Pip as an apprentice to his uncle—

not in making him a gentleman.

Pip reluctantly becomes Joe's apprentice, and time passes. One day, Pip learns that he has inherited a fortune from an anonymous benefactor—whom he supposes to be Miss Havisham. Pip leaves for London to begin his new life as a gentleman. Once there, he befriends Herbert, the son of his tutor, who explains the mystery behind Miss Havisham's eccentricities. Her house and attire have remained exactly the same as the moment she was jilted by her fiancé on the morning of their intended wedding day.

Pip gets swept up in his new life, becoming snobby toward the people from his past—including his uncle Joe—and truly believing that Miss Havisham intends for him to marry Estella.

When Pip is twenty-three he receives an unexpected visit

from the convict he encountered in the churchyard all of those years ago. It turns out that the convict, Magwitch, had made a fortune in Australia and, having never forgotten Pip's help, is actually Pip's benefactor. Pip is devastated by the realization that he is not intended to marry Estella. Nevertheless, he declares his love to her, only for her to inform him of her impending marriage to another suitor.

Despite his heartbreak, Pip turns his attention to helping Magwitch, who is being pursued by Compeyson, Magwitch's former partner in crime—and the former fiancé of Miss Havisham, who jilted her. Pip also discovers that Magwitch is Estella's father, and the realization that she is of even lower birth than himself sends Pip reeling.

Pip and Herbert attempt to help Magwitch escape London,

but they are caught. Not only is Pip's fortune confiscated, but Magwitch is found guilty and sentenced to death. Magwitch is at peace with his fate and dies believing that God has forgiven him. Grieving and no longer with an income, Pip narrowly escapes going to prison for his debts. After a thwarted attempt to start a new life back in Kent, Pip accepts a job working at Herbert's mercantile firm abroad.

Eleven years pass, and Pip is a bachelor. He returns to Kent to visit Joe and decides to take a walk in the unkempt gardens of Miss Havisham's estate. There, he encounters Estella, who is recently widowed. Pip concludes with "I saw no shadow of another parting from her."

Our Mutual Friend

(Serialized 1864–65)

"In these times of ours, though concerning the exact year there is no need to be precise, a boat of dirty and disreputable appearance, with two figures in it, floated on the Thames, between Southwark bridge which is of iron, and London Bridge which is of stone, as an autumn evening was closing in."

MAJOR CHARACTERS

John Harmon/Rokesmith: Heir to his father's fortune made from garbage.

The Boffins: Worked for John Harmon Sr. and second in line to inherit his estate.

Lizzie Hexman: The kind and beautiful daughter of a waterman.

Bella Wilford: Harmon Sr.'s will stipulates that his son must marry her in order to receive his inheritance.

Eugene Wrayburn: Snobbish barrister who takes a liking to Lizzie, despite her lowly station in life.

Bradley Headstone: Volatile headmaster who falls in love with Lizzie and is prepared to win her at any cost.

THE STORY

With John "dead," the elder Harmon's fortune is passed along to his good-natured foreman, Noddy Boffin. Boffin hires John Rokesmith as his secretary, but it doesn't take long for Boffin to realize that Rokesmith is the grown-up version of the boy they knew years ago. They don't let on that they know, though. Instead, they take in Bella Wilford, in order to facilitate

Rokesmith falling in love with her.

Meanwhile Gaffer Hexman is accused of murdering "John Harmon" but ends up drowning, himself. His orphaned daughter, Lizzie, has attracted a couple of suitors: arrogant barrister Eugene Wrayburn and Bradley Headstone, the pent-up schoolmaster of Lizzie's brother, Charley. Lizzie loves Wrayburn but feels that they can't be together because they are from different classes of society.

Headstone brutally attacks Wrayburn and leaves him for dead. Lizzie finds him and nurses him back to health and they are married. Headstone attempts to pin Wrayburn's attack on Roger "Rogue" Riderhood, the same man who accused Hexman of murdering John Harmon on the ship. Headstone and Riderhood end up quarreling, both falling into a lock and drowning.

Rokesmith falls in love with Bella and marries her—afterward revealing his true identity and claiming his inheritance.

The Mystery of Edwin Drood

(Serialized 1870—incomplete)

"An ancient English Cathedral Tower? How can the ancient English Cathedral tower be here! The well-known massive gray square tower of its old Cathedral? How can that be here! There is no spike of rusty iron in the air, between the eye and it, from any point of the real prospect."

MAJOR CHARACTERS

Edwin Drood: An orphan whose marriage was arranged by his father when he was a child.

John Jasper: Edwin's conniving, opium-addict uncle.

Rosa Bud: Edwin's intended, described as "wonderfully pretty, wonderfully childish, wonderfully whimsical."

Neville Landless: Orphan from Ceylon who harbors a secret crush on Rosa.

Helena Landless: Twin sister of Neville and best friend of Rosa.

THE STORY

Edwin Drood and Rosa Bud were betrothed to each other as children by their fathers. Both become orphaned, but they grow up with each other, aware of their arranged future together as husband and wife.

Edwin's guardian is his uncle, Jasper, who is a choirmaster addicted to opium and secretly in love with Rosa. Hiram Grewgious is Rosa's guardian who gives Edwin the ring (that once belonged to her mother) with which he is to propose— on the condition that he's entirely sure of his feelings for

Rosa. Edwin and Rosa meet and mutually decide to end their engagement, but keep the news to themselves for now.

Twins Helena and Neville Landless are orphans from Ceylon who have come to Cloisterham to be educated. Neville is smitten with Rosa and Helena becomes her good friend. Neville gets into a violent argument with Edwin, accusing him of not appreciating Rosa. After the quarrel, Edwin and Neville agree to meet for a peaceful Christmas Eve dinner at Jasper's house as a gesture of reconciliation. Neville has planned to leave on a two-week walking tour the following morning.

Christmas morning arrives, and Edwin is discovered to be missing. Neville is the immediate suspect and returns from his tour to declare his innocence. Since there is no evidence against him, he is not arrested.

Six months pass, and Jasper goes to Rosa to declare his love for her. Frightened, she flees to London to tell Grewgious what has happened. Rosa stays in London, and Helena keeps her company.

A mysterious stranger arrives and takes a good deal of interest in Jasper, following him around and even employing a local boy to keep tabs on him. . . .

Note: Only half of this final Dickens novel was completed at the time that Dickens suffered a stroke and died. From letters, it is clear he intended Jasper to be Edwin's murderer, but how the second half of the novel would have played out is indeed a mystery.

Credits:

This book has been bound
using handcraft methods
and Smyth-sewn
to ensure durability.

Designed by Bill Jones.

Written by Joelle Herr.

Edited by Cindy De La Hoz.

The text was set in
Adobe Caslon and
Caslon Antique.